DISNEY·PIXAR
MONSTERS, INC.
Scared Silly

◆ Book Five ◆

Disney PRESS

New York

AN IMPRINT OF DISNEY BOOK GROUP

"Hey, Sulley, you're number one!" a yellow monster called.

"You're the best!" another monster yelled.

The big blue monster's friends cheered for him. He and his best pal, Mike, were on their way to work at Monsters, Inc.

My pal is the best Scarer in all of Monstropolis, Mike, the one-eyed green monster, thought proudly.

At Monsters, Inc., it was the monsters' job to enter the human world so they could frighten children and gather screams. Then they brought the screams back to Monsters, Inc., where they were changed into energy. Sulley was the top Scarer.

Mike was a funny monster, though. He liked to make his friends laugh as he worked on the Scare Floor. He got things ready for Sulley before each assignment. They were a great team.

While Sulley did his warm-up scare exercises, Mike brought out a door to a child's room. He put a scream canister in place and waited for the light. As soon as it signaled, Sulley ran through the door.

Sulley crept into the child's room. *"Grrrr!"* he growled as the door closed.

"Aaaaaah!" Mike heard a kid scream.

"Wow, would you listen to that?" Mike said to the other monsters on the Scare Floor.

Mike was always amazed at how loudly kids screamed when they saw Sulley. Sometimes he wondered what it would be like to be a top Scarer.

That night, Mike talked to his girlfriend, Celia, about it. "Oh, Schmoopsie-Poo," she said, "you couldn't scare a flea!"

Celia had been trying to cheer Mike up, but she had just made him more determined to prove he could be scary—just like Sulley.

The next day, Mike came up with a plan.

When Sulley went through a door on the Scare Floor, Mike pulled a purple wig and two giant shoes with claws out of a bag.

Mike put on the outrageous costume and waited for Sulley to return.

As Sulley walked through the door, Mike shouted, *"Boo!"*

"Aaaaaah!" Sulley yelled and tripped over Mike's shoes. "Why'd you do that?" he asked.

"Did I scare you?" Mike asked.

"No, you surprised me," Sulley replied.

"Oh." Mike was disappointed, but he wasn't going to give up.

That night, Mike left work without Sulley. As Sulley headed home alone, he wondered why his pal hadn't waited for him. He entered their apartment and heard a strange wailing noise.

Suddenly, Mike jumped out. He was covered in spaghetti and tomato sauce. "I'm a noodle monster!" he screeched loudly.

Sulley couldn't stop laughing.

Mike had been sure the noodle monster would be frightening, but Sulley just thought it was a joke.

"I guess that means you weren't scared," Mike said.

When Sulley calmed down, he replied, "Scared? You are one great jokester, Mike!"

Mike stomped into his bedroom and closed the door.

Sulley stood outside. "Come on, Mike. Open up!" he called, knocking on the door.

"Go away," Mike answered.

Later, Sulley ate dinner by himself. He didn't understand why Mike had gotten so angry. He missed spending time with him, though.

Sulley decided he would apologize in the morning. He wasn't sure what he'd done, but he didn't want Mike to be mad.

The next morning, when Sulley woke up, Mike had already left. Well, so much for apologizing, Sulley thought. He walked to work by himself and wondered why Mike was acting so strangely. Mike was usually such a happy-go-lucky monster. Maybe he was sick or had a fight with Celia.

Sulley went to the locker room to get ready. But he didn't feel like doing his job. He was too worried about his friend.

When he opened his locker door, Mike jumped out. He was covered with blue and purple fur, just like Sulley. He even wore stilts to make himself tall. *"Grrrrr!"* Mike yelled loudly, waving his arms.

Sulley was surprised.

"Aw, Mike, what's wrong with you?" Sulley asked. "Why are you making fun of me? I thought you were my friend."

"*Grrrr!*" Mike responded. Surely, Sulley must have been scared, he thought.

Sulley's feelings were really hurt. He frowned and started to walk to the Scare Floor. Mike clumped after him on his stilts. "Stop! Come back, Sulley!" he yelled. "Look at me! I'm scary, like you!"

All the other monsters began to follow Mike and Sulley. They wanted to see what Mike would do next.

"What a joker!" they shouted. "Mike, you're the funniest! We're going to bust our guts laughing!"

Mike was annoyed. He wanted the other monsters to think he was scary, not funny. He took a huge breath. "Watch this!" he called.

"*Rrrrrr!*" Mike roared. He waved his arms menacingly, but the others just smiled.

"*Rrrrrr!*" he repeated. The other monsters chuckled. Mike wondered why no one looked frightened. That was the loudest, scariest sound he'd ever made.

Then Mike's stilts flew out from under him. "*Eeeeee!*" he yelled.

Thud! Mike groaned as he hit the floor. "*Ow, ow, ow, ow!*" he cried as he bounced along.

All the monsters laughed as Mike finally rolled to a stop beside Sulley's gigantic feet. Mike sat up and rubbed his head.

"What are you trying to do?" Sulley asked.

"I wanted to see if I could scare someone," Mike explained. "But I'm no good at it." He looked down sadly. "See! Everyone is just laughing. Nobody looks frightened."

Sulley helped his pal stand up. "Look, Mike, that's what everyone likes about you. You make them laugh," he said. "Besides, you sure had me scared!"

"Oh, sure," Mike grumbled. "How?"

"Well, I thought you were going to quit being my best pal," Sulley answered. "And that's just about the scariest thing I could ever imagine."

Mike gently punched Sulley's arm as the two friends began walking down the hall.

"Quit being your best pal?" Mike asked. "Aw, Sulley, don't make me laugh!"